BLACK PANTHER

WARRIORS OF WAKANDA

By Frank Berrios
Illustrated by Simone Buonfantino,
Davide Mastrolonardo, and Fabio Paciulli

 A GOLDEN BOOK • NEW YORK

 © 2018 MARVEL marvelkids.com

All rights reserved. Published in the United States by Golden Books, an imprint of Random House
Children's Books, a division of Penguin Random House LLC, 1745 Broadway, New York, NY 10019, and in
Canada by Penguin Random House Canada Limited, Toronto. Golden Books, A Golden Book, A Little Golden
Book, the G colophon, and the distinctive gold spine are registered trademarks of Penguin Random House LLC.
rhcbooks.com
ISBN 978-1-9848-3172-9 (trade) — ISBN 978-1-9848-3184-2 (ebook)
Printed in the United States of America
10 9 8 7 6 5 4 3 2 1

T'CHALLA IS THE KING of the African nation Wakanda. Most of the world knows him as the super hero **Black Panther!** He uses his amazing strength and speed to protect his people and the powerful metal Vibranium.

But T'Challa doesn't protect Wakanda by himself. **Okoye** is the leader of the Dora Milaje. These fierce female warriors protect Wakanda and their king at all times.

Ayo assists Okoye in her missions with Black Panther!

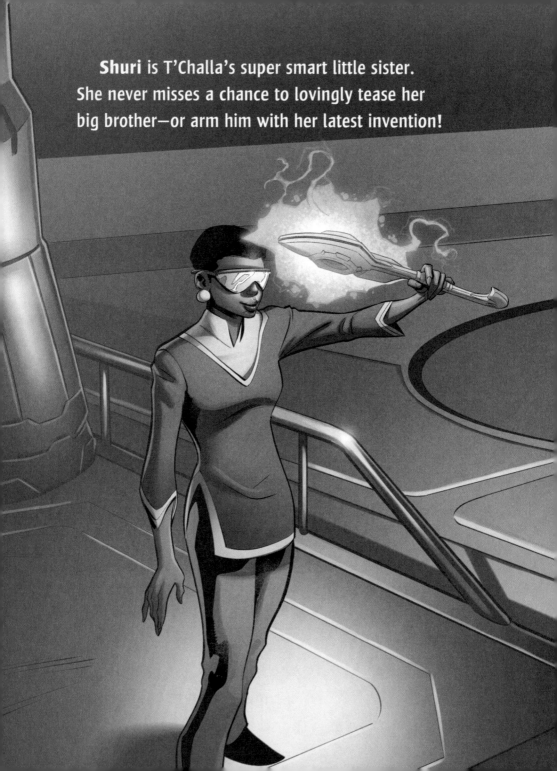

Shuri is T'Challa's super smart little sister. She never misses a chance to lovingly tease her big brother—or arm him with her latest invention!

Ramonda is T'Challa's wise mother.
Her love and advice help him rule Wakanda.

Wakanda is a peaceful kingdom, but when troubles arise, the Dora Milaje race to T'Challa's side!

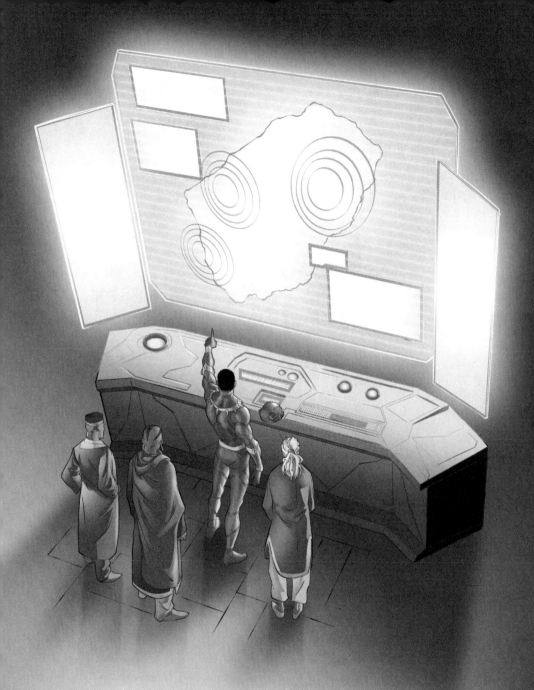

Wakanda's advanced technology allows
them to quickly locate any problem.

Being a king and a leader is not easy. Black Panther listens to the community's elders and his trusted advisors. With their help, he makes decisions—and then, with his fearless friends, he goes wherever he is needed!

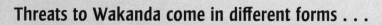

Threats to Wakanda come in different forms . . .

. . . and sometimes, super villains attack. These bad guys want Wakanda's valuable Vibranium and technology for themselves!

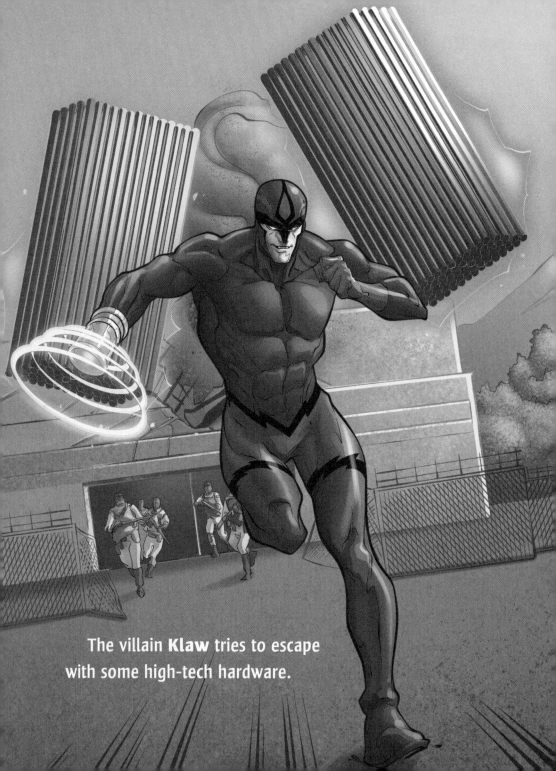

The villain **Klaw** tries to escape
with some high-tech hardware.

Klaw doesn't get far—
Black Panther pursues him.

Black Panther faces Klaw. And he doesn't fight alone. . . .

Shuri, Okoye, and Ayo arrive! Shuri uses
the energy emitter she invented—*ZZZwap!*
It throws Klaw off-balance.

Okoye and Ayo race into battle. They are
ready to fight if Klaw won't surrender peacefully!

Klaw is no match for the brave warriors of Wakanda!
Working together, they quickly take down the villain.

T'Challa smiles at Shuri—teamwork wins again!

The crowd cheers when Black Panther
and the Dora Milaje return to the palace.

T'Challa's mother proudly greets him—the hero and king.

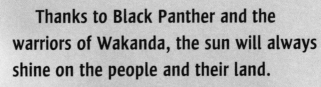

Thanks to Black Panther and the warriors of Wakanda, the sun will always shine on the people and their land.

WAKANDA FOREVER!